Allah Gave Me Two Eyes to See…

by FATIMA M. D'OYEN

illustrated by STEVAN STRATFORD

THE ISLAMIC FOUNDATION

For Daliah, Alyssa and Emani with love

The Islamic Foundation would like to gratefully acknowledge the efforts of Anwar Cara for developing the ALLAH THE MAKER SERIES *concept, Noura Durkee and Michèle Messaoudi for editing, and Dr Manazir Ahsan for his general encouragement and support.*

© The Islamic Foundation 1998/1418H

ISBN 0 86037 283 9

MUSLIM CHILDREN'S LIBRARY

ALLAH GAVE ME TWO EYES TO SEE...
Author: Fatima M. D'Oyen
Illustrator: Stevan Stratford

Published by
The Islamic Foundation, Markfield Conference Centre, Ratby Lane, Markfield, Leicester LE67 9SY, United Kingdom
Tel: (01530) 244944 Fax: (01530) 244946 E-Mail: i-foundation@islamic-foundation.org.uk

Quran House, PO Box 30611, Nairobi, Kenya

PMB 3193, Kano, Nigeria

Printed by Proost International Book Production, Belgium

Allah gave me two eyes to see…

the shiny green leaves
of plants and trees

the black of night
the white of snow

and the colours
of the bright rainbow

the tall grey buildings
and the tiny brown bee

*Allah gave me
two eyes to see*

Allah gave me two ears to hear…

the humming-bird
humming
as it draws near

the evening stillness
so quiet and clear

the noisy dog's bark
as we walk in the park

my father's loud
sneeze and the
whispering breeze

the tea kettle singing
the door bell ringing

*Allah gave me
two ears to hear*

Allah gave me a tongue to taste...

chocolate cake so fun to bake!

sour cherries
and sweet blueberries

salty chips
and spicy dips

cold ice cream
that we eat in haste

*Allah gave me
a tongue to taste*

Allah gave me a nose to smell…

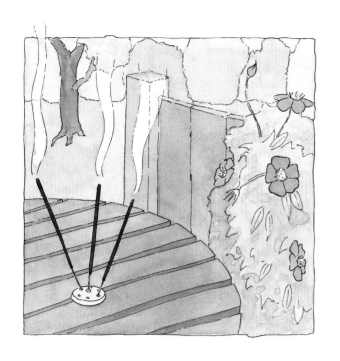

sweet incense and
flowers around
the fence

burning leaves
and pepper that
makes me sneeze

good food cooking, while I wait looking!

in the bakery,
the buns they sell

*Allah gave me
a nose to smell*

Allah gave me my skin to feel…

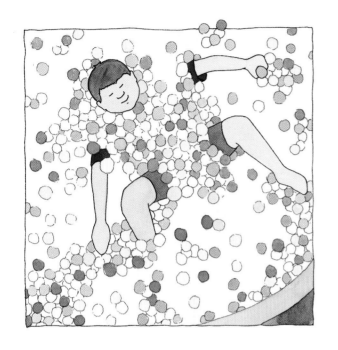

with fingers and toes,
elbows and heels

slippery soap
and sticky gum

my kitten's soft
fur and his rough,
tickly tongue

bark on trees
and scrapes on knees

my mother's hands
made to heal

*Allah gave me
my skin to feel*

Allah gave me...

a mind to think and a heart to love

and thank Him for His gifts from above

a mouth to smile
and praise Him
all the while

Subhan-Allah!
Glory to Allah!
Al-Hamdu-lillah!
Praise to Allah!
Allahu Akbar!
Allah is the Greatest!